Sadie and the Snowman

by
Allen Morgan

illustrated by Brenda Clark

KIDS CAN PRESS

To Joan and Len

Kids Can Press gratefully acknowledges the assistance of the Canada Council and the Ontario Arts Council in the production of this book.

Canadian Cataloguing in Publication Data

Morgan, Allen, 1946–
Sadie and the snowman

ISBN 0-919964-86-9 (bound). –
0-919964-78-8 (pbk.).

I. Clark, Brenda.   II. Title.

PS8576.073S34 1985 jc813'.54 C85-098460-2
PZ7.M67Sa 1985

Book design by Wycliffe Smith
Printed by Everbest Printing Co. Ltd., Hong Kong.

85 0

Sadie and the Snowman

One cold winter day, Sadie made a snowman in her back yard. First she made a snowball and then she made two more. Then she rolled them and rolled them until they were done.

She used cookies for the eyes, an apple for the nose, and a great big banana for the smile.

He was a really good snowman and he lasted for a long time.

But some birds ate the cookies, a squirrel ate the apple, and a large raccoon stole the banana. The sun came out and the snowman began to melt. After a while he didn't look much like a snowman at all.

Sadie was sad. She missed the snowman. So the next time it snowed, she made the snowman all over again.

There was still a bit of the snowman left, so she made it into a snowball. Then she made two more, and she rolled them and rolled them until they were done. She used crackers for the eyes, a carrot for the nose, and a nice fat zucchini for the smile.

He was a really good snowman and he lasted for a long time.

But the birds ate the crackers, the squirrel ate the carrot, and a large raccoon stole the zucchini. The sun came out and the snowman began to melt. After a while he didn't look much like a snowman at all.

This time Sadie wasn't sad. She knew it would snow again.

All that winter Sadie made the snowman over and over again. The birds ate the eyes, the squirrel ate the noses, and a large raccoon stole all the smiles. The sun kept coming out and the snowman kept melting. But there was always enough of the snowman left to start all over again.

Then the weather turned warmer. The sun came out earlier and it stayed out longer. Sadie worried about the snowman. She found an old blanket and made him a tent so he could hide from the sun. But the wind began to blow, and it blew and blew until finally one day the tent flew away.

Spring was coming and the snow on the ground was melting so fast that the grass grew through. The snowman was melting too. Sadie took him apart and moved him under the porch where the sun couldn't see him. But even so, he kept getting smaller. After a while he didn't look much like a snowman at all.

The weather turned colder again just in time. It snowed a little during the night, and in the morning Sadie made the snowman again. There was still a bit of the snowman left, so she made it into a snowball. Then she made two more, and she rolled them and rolled them until they were done. She used raisins for the eyes, a peanut for the nose, and a twist of red licorice for the smile. When the snowman was finished, Sadie put him into a bowl and moved him back under the porch.

He was a really good snowman, but Sadie wasn't sure how long he would last this time.

The birds ate the raisins, the squirrel ate the peanut, and a large raccoon stole the licorice. The sun came out and the weather turned warm again. This time the snowman melted down all the way and all that was left was a bowl full of water.

Sadie was sad. The really good snowman was gone now for good, and she knew she would miss him.

Then Sadie smiled. She knew just what to do. She poured all the water out of the bowl and into a plastic bag. Then she put the plastic bag into her freezer.

And for all that summer and all that fall, Sadie didn't miss the snowman at all. She knew she would see him again.

So when winter came and it snowed again, Sadie took the plastic bag from her freezer and went outside. First she made a snowball all around the ice she had saved. Then she made two more, and she rolled them and rolled them until they were done. She used cookies for the eyes, an apple for the nose, and a great big banana for the smile.

He was a really good snowman and he lasted for a long time.

KIDS CAN PRESS

$4.95